Clever Cat

by Karen Wallace and Anni Axworthy

FRANKLIN WATTS
LONDON • SYDNEY

Clever Cat

First published in 2003 by
Franklin Watts
96 Leonard Street
London
EC2A 4XD

Franklin Watts Australia
45–51 Huntley Street
Alexandria
NSW 2015

A CIP catalogue record for this book is available
from the British Library.

ISBN 0 7496 4890 2 (hbk)
ISBN 0 7496 5131 8 (pbk)

Series Editor: Jackie Hamley
Series Advisor: Dr Barrie Wade
Cover Design: Jason Anscomb
Design: Peter Scoulding

Printed in Hong Kong / China

For Dave the cat – KW

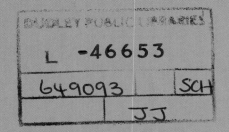

Clever Cat dances with his head in the air. "I've got a tail like a wolf," he cries. "My eyes are green as a dragon!"

Old Mother Goose
waggles her wings.

Nanny Goat rolls
her strange eyes.

"You're a silly young cat,"
quacks Mr Duck. "You should
be out catching mice.

8

You should be out hunting rats.
Not dancing about with your head
in the air!"

9

Clever Cat grins. He doesn't care.
"You're a bunch of old fusspots,"
he cries. And he tickles their noses
as he swishes his tail.

"I'm telling the farmer!" squawks
Old Mother Goose.

Nanny Goat nods and blows through her nose. "What good is a cat with a tail like a wolf?"

Mr Duck shakes his fine feathered head. "Who cares if his eyes are as green as a dragon?"

That night, a huge moon rises over the farmyard. Tucked up in bed, the farmer snores and turns over.

He doesn't see the hungry fox trot
over the meadow. He doesn't hear
the gate creak and swing open.

Clever Cat is awake.

He hides in the shadows.

He sees the hungry fox
creep over the farmyard.

Old Mother Goose shivers and shakes. The goat and the duck huddle beside her.

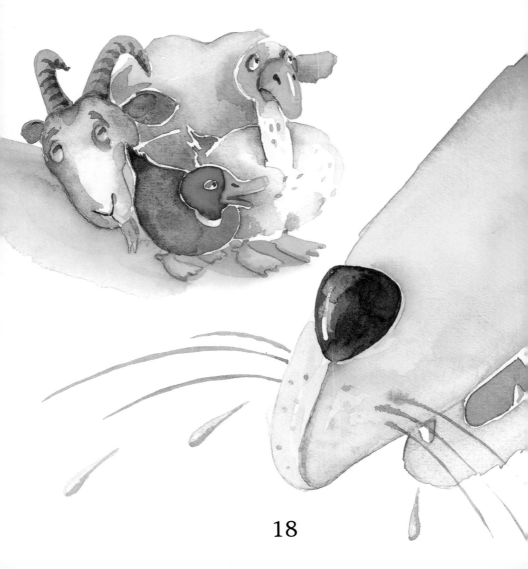

They want to run from the fox,
but they are frozen like statues.

19

The hungry fox drools. He creeps closer and closer. Will he eat...

...a goose,

or a goat,

or a duck

for his supper?

Clever Cat jumps! In the glow of the moon, his tail is huge like a wolf.

By the light of the stars, his eyes
are green like a dragon.

"Help!" cries the fox. "It's a wolf!

It's a dragon!

His heart bangs in his chest.

His legs tremble like jelly.

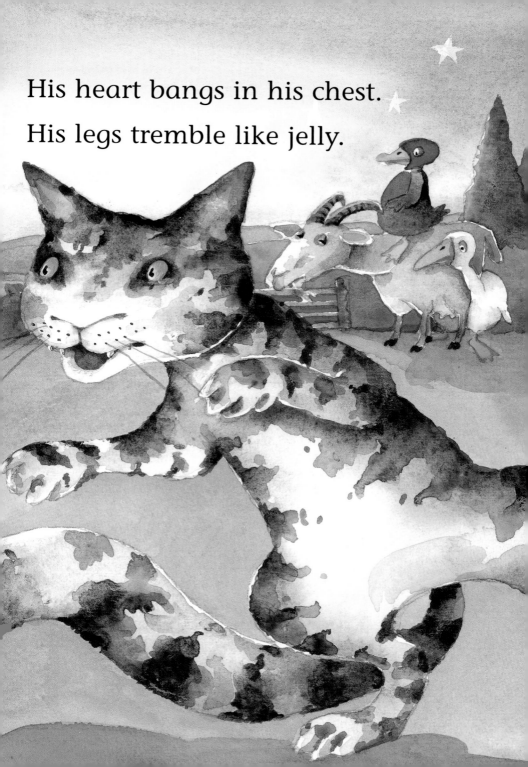

The frightened
fox turns and
runs from the
farmyard.

Old Mother Goose waggles her wings. Nanny Goat blinks her strange eyes.

"You're a wonder, you are," quacks
Mr Duck. "We're sorry we called
you a silly young cat."

29

Clever Cat grins. He doesn't care.
He dances about with his head
in the air!

Hopscotch has been specially designed to fit the requirements of the National Literacy Strategy. It offers real books by top authors and illustrators for children developing their reading skills.

There are 14 other Hopscotch stories to choose from:

This igloo book belongs to:

....

Published in 2013
by Igloo Books Ltd
Cottage Farm
Sywell
NN6 0BJ
www.igloobooks.com

SHE001 1113
2 4 6 8 10 9 7 5 3
ISBN 978-0-85780-857-8

Printed and manufactured in China

My Treasury of Princess Stories

igloobooks

Contents

Snow White

Long ago, there lived a king and queen who were overjoyed when they had a beautiful, baby girl. However, soon after the child was born, the queen died. The poor king was heartbroken. He held his baby daughter and looked at her. She had lips as red as blood, hair as black as night and skin as white as snow. "I shall name you Snow White," said the king.

A few years later, the king married again. Snow White's stepmother was beautiful, but also very cruel and vain. She was secretly a witch, who had great powers. The new queen owned a magic mirror, which answered any question that was asked of it.

Each day, Snow White's stepmother always asked the mirror the same question, "Mirror, mirror, on the wall, who is the fairest of them all?" The mirror always replied with the same answer, "You, my queen, are the fairest of them all."

This made the queen very happy. Secretly, she was jealous of Snow White and feared that the girl would grow to be more beautiful than herself.

One day, when Snow White had grown into a young woman, the queen asked the mirror her usual question, "Mirror, mirror, on the wall, who is the fairest of them all?"
This time, the mirror replied, "Snow White is the fairest of them all."

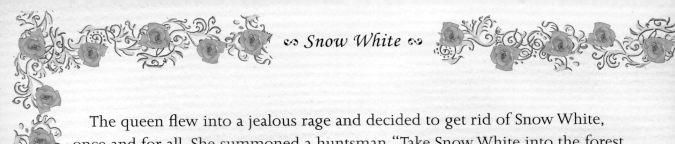

The queen flew into a jealous rage and decided to get rid of Snow White, once and for all. She summoned a huntsman. "Take Snow White into the forest and kill her!" she commanded. The huntsman didn't want to kill Snow White but, like everyone else in the castle, he was terrified of the wicked queen.

That night, the huntsman grabbed Snow White from her bed while she was sleeping, and took her into the dark, dangerous forest. Even though the huntsman was cowardly, he wasn't evil and he couldn't kill Snow White. Instead, he put her down safely in the middle of the forest and warned her not to return to the castle.

Snow White wandered through the forest all night, getting more and more tired and frightened. As the first light of day broke through the twisted trees, she found a strange little cottage. She knocked, but nobody answered.

Entering, she found seven little plates around a table, with seven little chairs and seven little beds in the corner. Snow White was so tired she lay on a bed and went to sleep.

When she awoke, Snow White saw seven dwarfs staring at her. At first, the dwarfs were angry that Snow White had come into their home. However, when Snow White explained her troubles, they said that she could stay. So Snow White lived in the little cottage with the seven dwarfs.

Meanwhile, the evil queen asked the mirror if she was the fairest of them all. "Snow White is the fairest of them all," replied the mirror. The jealous queen was furious and asked the mirror where Snow White was. The mirror told her about the little cottage, deep in the forest.

The queen used magic to disguise herself as an old woman. The next day, when the dwarfs were working, the queen went to the cottage with an armful of pretty clothes. "Try this pretty dress on, my dear," she cackled. Snow White tried the dress on, but the queen laced it up so tightly that Snow White could not breathe. She fell to the ground and lay still. The queen fled before the dwarfs could return. She was sure that Snow White was dead.

That evening, the dwarfs returned to the cottage and found Snow White. They quickly unlaced the deadly dress and Snow White was able to breathe again. The dwarfs were relieved that no harm had come to their friend.

That night, the queen questioned the magic mirror again, only to find out that Snow White was still alive. This time, her rage was terrible to see. She enchanted an apple so that one side was full of deadly poison, but the other was safe to eat. The only thing that could break the spell was a kiss from Snow White's true love.

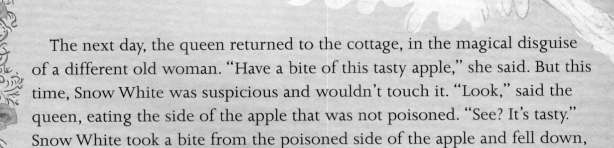

The next day, the queen returned to the cottage, in the magical disguise of a different old woman. "Have a bite of this tasty apple," she said. But this time, Snow White was suspicious and wouldn't touch it. "Look," said the queen, eating the side of the apple that was not poisoned. "See? It's tasty." Snow White took a bite from the poisoned side of the apple and fell down, as if dead.

This time, when the dwarfs returned, they couldn't wake Snow White. "She's dead!" they shouted. The dwarfs were very sad. They made Snow White a magnificent glass coffin and cried as they laid her in it.

Long years passed and the dwarfs guarded the coffin every day. Snow White stayed as beautiful as ever, as if she were only asleep.

One fine day, a handsome prince passed by the house and saw Snow White in the coffin. He fell in love immediately. "Who is this beautiful girl?" he asked. "I must kiss her." He opened the coffin and kissed the girl's cheek. As he did, Snow White awoke. True love's kiss had broken the curse.

The prince took Snow White to his palace and they were married straight away. Snow White asked the seven dwarfs to join them and they all lived happily ever after.

Cinderella

Once upon a time, there was a man who had a beautiful wife and a lovely daughter, called Ella. When his wife died, the man married another woman, who had two daughters of her own. They became Ella's step-sisters, but they were jealous of her and treated her like a servant. Poor Ella had to wear old, tatty clothes and do all the housework.

One day, Ella was in the kitchen, cleaning out the grate, when the two step-sisters came to see her. Ella's ragged clothes were stained and her face was covered in soot. "Look how dirty she is," crowed one sister, fluttering her fan. "She's covered with ashes and cinders."
"We should call her Cinder-Ella!" said the other sister.
From that moment on, Ella became known as Cinderella.

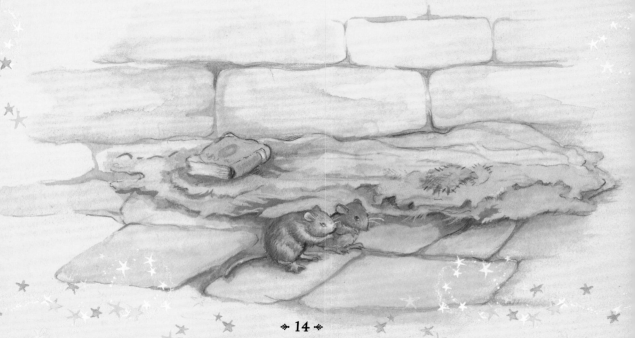

One day, news arrived at the house that the prince of the land was going to hold a Grand Ball at the palace. Cinderella's father made sure that his new wife, as well as Cinderella and her two step-sisters, were invited. But when the invitations came, the sisters tore up Cinderella's before she saw it.

"Too bad," they said, "the prince doesn't want you in his beautiful palace."

When the night of the ball came, Cinderella had to help her step-mother and her step-sisters dress in their fancy gowns. Then she was sent back to the kitchen, to do all the washing, while they left for the ball. When all the work was done, Cinderella sat in the cold kitchen and cried. "I'm so sad and lonely," she said, "won't anyone help me?"

The chimney of the big kitchen fireplace began to glow and sparkle, then something bright rushed out. A twinkling, fizzing light circled the kitchen and a kind-looking fairy appeared, in a shower of sparks.

"Who are you?" asked Cinderella, in surprise.

"I'm your Fairy Godmother," answered the fairy, "and you look in need of help. What can I do for you?"

Cinderella explained that she wasn't allowed to go to the Grand Ball.

"Don't worry," said the Fairy Godmother, "you shall go to the ball!"

"But how can I go dressed in these rags?" asked Cinderella.

"A little magic will fix that," said the Fairy Godmother, sweetly. She waved her wand around Cinderella's head and her rags fluttered and flapped and swished and swelled, until they had turned into the most amazing ballgown Cinderella had ever seen. It even had a pair of glass slippers to match.

"Of course, you'll need to get to the ball," added the Fairy Godmother. She waved her wand over a pumpkin and it became a magnificent, sparkly, gold coach. Cinderella was amazed and thrilled to see the wonderful coach.

Next, the Fairy Godmother searched around the garden and found a lizard and four mice. She waved her wand over them and they were transformed into a coachman and four beautiful horses. "Now you can go to the ball," said the Fairy Godmother. "But remember, all my magic stops at midnight. So make sure that you are back here before then."

When Cinderella entered the ball at the palace all eyes were upon her.
The handsome prince took one look at her and fell instantly in love. He spent
every minute of the night dancing with her.

Cinderella enjoyed herself so much she forgot to watch the big clock that
hung at one end of the ballroom. "I am falling in love with you," the prince
told Cinderella, as they danced.

"Do you love me because of my fine clothes?" asked Cinderella.

"I would love you, even if you were in rags," said the prince.

Suddenly, the clock began to strike midnight. Terrified of showing herself in her dirty rags, Cinderella broke free of the prince and ran out of the palace. In her haste, she left behind one of her glass slippers. As she was running down the palace steps, the gown turned back into rags, the coach became a pumpkin again and the rats and lizard scuttled away. Cinderella ran back to her house and nobody knew that she had ever left it.

The prince swore that he would find the owner of the slipper. "The girl whose foot fits this slipper is the girl I shall marry," he said. The prince and his pages visited every house in the land and every girl, in every house, tried on the slipper. But it was so small and dainty, nobody's foot would fit into it.

At last, the prince came to Cinderella's house. "He mustn't see you," her step-mother said, so the sisters locked Cinderella in the coal cellar to hide her from the prince. The two sisters both tried to make the shoe fit but, no matter how hard they squeezed, they couldn't squash their big feet into the tiny, delicate, glass slipper.

The prince was ready to leave when he heard knocking coming from the cellar door. Opening it, he was surprised to see a young girl dressed in rags and covered in ash and coal dust. "Let this girl try on the slipper," said the prince.

Cinderella tried the slipper on and her little foot slipped into it perfectly. The prince knew immediately that Cinderella was the girl he had danced with at the palace. "Will you marry me and be my queen?" asked the prince.

Cinderella had never felt so happy and accepted joyfully. The prince banished the wicked step-mother and the step-sisters to a faraway land and Cinderella and the prince married without delay. Cinderella's father came to live with them in the prince's palace and all three of them lived happily ever after.

Rapunzel

Once upon a time, a poor couple lived next door to an enchantress. The enchantress had a garden full of fruit and vegetables. Every year, all the delicious carrots, lettuces and apples lay on the ground and rotted. Meanwhile, the poor couple had hardly enough to eat.

One day, the poor man's wife was very hungry indeed. She was about to have a baby and needed to eat some food. Her husband climbed the wall and went into the enchantress' garden. He picked a big lettuce and took some juicy apples and carrots home to his wife.

The man and his wife ate the food and it was delicious. But the enchantress was very angry with the poor couple. "You have stolen from me," she said. "When your baby is born, I will take it from you."

Sure enough, when the man's wife gave birth to a baby girl the wicked enchantress came to take her away.

The child, who the enchantress named Rapunzel, grew into a lovely young woman, with long, golden hair. She had a beautiful singing voice and even though the enchantress hated to hear her, Rapunzel sang all day long.

One day, the enchantress took Rapunzel to a tall tower in the middle of a forest. She cast a spell on the tower, so that anyone left alone in it could never escape. "This spell cannot be undone," cackled the enchantress. "You will live here forever and I will not have to listen to you sing!"

Sometimes, the enchantress came to visit Rapunzel. She would call out, "Rapunzel, Rapunzel, let down your hair." Rapunzel would unpin her long, golden hair and lower it out of the window, so the enchantress could climb up into the tower room. The enchantress gave Rapunzel a few scraps of food and made sure that nobody had managed to enter the tower. Then she would climb back down Rapunzel's hair and scurry home.

One morning, a prince was wandering through the forest and heard Rapunzel singing. He was entranced by her beautiful voice and followed it to the tower. He saw the enchantress call out, "Rapunzel, Rapunzel, let down your hair," and then climb up the golden locks.

When the enchantress had left, the prince called out, "Rapunzel, Rapunzel, let down your hair." Rapunzel, thinking the enchantress had returned, shook her hair out the window and the prince climbed up.

Rapunzel was very surprised to see a handsome prince instead of the enchantress. Rapunzel and the prince fell in love and the prince vowed to rescue her. "I will visit you every night and bring you silk to weave into a ladder, so you can climb down the tower," the prince promised.

Night after night, the prince brought more and more silk to the tower. It was such fine material that Rapunzel could hide it in her dress, so the enchantress did not see it when she came to visit. But the enchantress was clever. She saw that Rapunzel was happy and she did not know why. She asked Rapunzel many questions, but didn't get any answers.

The enchantress became angry and grabbed Rapunzel by her dress. The silk came flying out in a long, billowing wave. "Wretch!" cried the enchantress. "You have tried my patience long enough!" The enchantress grabbed her scissors and cut off Rapunzel's long, golden hair. Then she muttered a spell and Rapunzel found herself far from the tower, in an unknown land, with no food, or water, and no way to reach her prince.

Meanwhile, the enchantress waited in the tower for the prince to arrive. That night, he called out softly, "Rapunzel, Rapunzel, let down your hair." The enchantress lowered Rapunzel's hair. The prince climbed up to find the furious enchantress waiting for him.
"So, you're the one who tried to steal my Rapunzel, are you?" she sneered.

The prince tried to grab the enchantress, but she pushed him backwards and he toppled out of the window, pulling Rapunzel's hair down with him. The prince landed in some bushes at the foot of the tower. He looked up at the enchantress who was shaking her fist and screaming with rage. She was alone in the tower and her spell could not be undone. The evil enchantress was trapped by her own magic.

The prince set off to look for Rapunzel. He wandered far and wide, searching towns and villages along the way. The prince often heard people talk of a girl with a beautiful voice, but no matter how hard he looked, he could never find her.

After many disappointments the prince had almost given up hope when one day he heard the sweet, familiar sound of Rapunzel singing. She had found work on a farm and was singing sadly as she carried water from the well. The prince ran to Rapunzel and they embraced.

The prince took Rapunzel home to see her parents. They were overjoyed at the return of their daughter. Soon after, the prince married Rapunzel and they lived happily ever after. As for the enchantress, she was trapped in the tower for the rest of her days and never troubled anyone, ever again.

Beauty and the Beast

Once, there was a poor merchant who had three lovely daughters. The youngest daughter was the kindest and most beautiful. Her name was Belle and she loved her father dearly.

One day, when the merchant had to go on a long journey, he asked his daughters what presents they would like him to bring back. The older sisters asked for dresses and jewels, but Belle knew that her father was poor and could not afford such finery. "I only want a rose, Father," she said.

The merchant journeyed far and wide. On the way back to his village, he was caught in a tremendous storm. Seeking shelter, he found a glittering palace. Nobody seemed to be in the palace, not even the humblest servant. Every one of the huge rooms was empty. The merchant sat down to rest and saw that a table was being magically laid for him. The plates and food flew through the air, as if they were being carried by invisible hands. The surprised merchant ate a hearty meal, then decided to continue on his way.

As he was leaving the palace, he saw a rose bush and remembered his promise to Belle. The merchant reached out and picked a single, red rose. Suddenly, there was a crash of thunder and a horrible beast appeared.

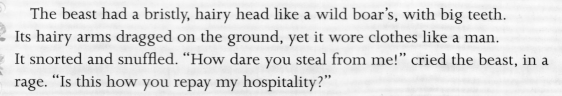

The beast had a bristly, hairy head like a wild boar's, with big teeth. Its hairy arms dragged on the ground, yet it wore clothes like a man. It snorted and snuffled. "How dare you steal from me!" cried the beast, in a rage. "Is this how you repay my hospitality?"

The merchant said he was very sorry and explained that he was only picking the rose for his daughter. But the beast wouldn't be calmed. "To pay for your crime, you must send this daughter to live with me. If you do not, I will come for you and take your life!"

The merchant hurried home and told his family what had happened. "I must go to the beast, or it will kill you," said Belle, sadly. The merchant wouldn't let Belle leave, but that night, she climbed out of her bedroom window and walked all the way to the palace by herself.

The beast was waiting for her. At first, Belle was terrified by the sight of such an ugly monster, but the beast bowed and welcomed her politely. The invisible servants prepared them a delicious meal and they ate together. "This palace is your new home," grunted the beast. "There are many delights for you here. And now, I have a question to ask you. Will you marry me?"

Belle was shocked. "I can't marry you. I've only just met you," she said. The beast didn't look angry, he just nodded sadly and left.

That night, as Belle slept, she dreamed of a handsome prince. The prince seemed to be calling to her. "Save me! Please save me!" he cried.

The next day, Belle explored the palace. It was beautiful and magical. The invisible servants fetched her any food and drink she asked for. Every room was filled with beautiful dresses, gold, jewels and all manner of fine objects.

Every evening, Belle and the beast would eat together and the beast would always ask Belle the same question. "Will you marry me?"

But Belle always refused. Even though she couldn't dream of marrying such a hideous monster, she grew to love the beast. He gave her anything she asked for and in return, she was able to soften his rough manners and calm his dreadful temper.

Every night, Belle dreamt of the handsome prince. She would ask how she could save him, but the prince would only say, "Don't trust appearances." There was something about the prince's eyes that reminded her of someone. But try as she might, she couldn't think who it was.

As the months passed, Belle began to miss her family. One night, she asked the beast if she could visit them for a while. "I cannot refuse you," said the beast, "but I love you so much, if you do not return soon, I shall die." The beast gave her a magic ring which transported her back home to her father and sisters.

Belle was so glad to see her family that she spent many days in their company. She almost forgot about the palace and the beast, until one night she had another dream. This time, it was the beast she saw, lying in the palace, almost dead from grief. "I have been so cruel!" cried Belle. She touched the magic ring and, in a flash, it transported her back to the palace in the blink of an eye.

Belle ran down the marble corridors and found the beast, just as he had been in her dream. He was lying on the floor, unmoving. She ran to him and cried, trying to wake him up. When her tears fell on his bristly face, he opened his eyes. "It is too late for me," he said. "I think I am going to die. Goodbye, Belle. It's a shame you didn't want to marry me."
"I will marry you, Beast!" cried Belle, hugging him tightly.

The moment she said the words, Belle felt the beast begin to change. He stumbled away and turned from her and when he turned back, he was no longer a beast. In his place was the handsome prince from her dreams.

The prince smiled at her. "I was cursed by a wicked witch to be a beast," he explained. "I have lived alone for many years, too afraid to go into the outside world because of my ugliness. The only way to break the curse was to find someone pure enough of heart to marry me, even though I was so horrible to look at."

Suddenly, all the servants became visible around him and they cheered the happy couple. The prince used the magic ring to bring Belle's father and her sisters to the castle. Soon after, the prince and Belle were married and they lived happily ever after.

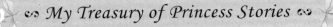

Sleeping Beauty

Once upon a time, a baby girl was born to a king and queen. She looked so bright and fair, they decided to name her 'Beauty' and a great celebration was held in her honour.

Because the queen was half-fairy, she invited three of her fairy cousins to give blessings to the baby. However, she forgot to invite one distant relative – a fairy with a very bad temper.

On the day of the blessings, the fairies gathered round the child's crib. "I give Beauty the gift of goodness and kindness," said the first fairy. "I give Beauty the gift of graceful dancing," said the second fairy.

Before the third fairy could utter her blessing, a cold wind whirled around the crib. The angry fairy, who had not been invited, appeared. Her face was like thunder. "So, you're having a blessing without me?" she snarled, "Now this child will have my present, whether you like it or not! I curse Beauty to prick her finger on her sixteenth birthday and die!" Suddenly, the wind whirled again and the fairy vanished.

Everyone was too shocked to speak. Finally, the third fairy spoke. "I have not given my gift yet," she said in a small voice. "It is not within my power to lift the curse laid on Beauty, but I can change it a little. My gift to you, Beauty, is this – you will not die on your sixteenth birthday, but you will sleep for a hundred years, until you are awakened by true love's first kiss."

Beauty grew up to be a wonderful girl, full of the fairy gifts of kindness and grace. However, she always wondered why no sharp objects were allowed in the castle and why she was never allowed outside. She ate with a spoon, instead of a knife and fork, and she never learned to spin, or sew. Her royal parents were terrified in case Beauty should prick her finger and fall asleep.

On the day of her sixteenth birthday, Beauty was exploring the castle. In one corner of the Great Hall, she saw a little door that she had never noticed before. It led up a winding staircase, to a room in the highest tower. There, Beauty saw a woman sitting by a spinning wheel.

Beauty greeted the woman and asked what she was doing. "I'm spinning," replied the woman, who was the angry fairy in disguise. "Would you like to try spinning, my child?"

"Yes, please," said Beauty and she sat at the spinning wheel. The fairy passed Beauty a sharp spindle, to wind the thread. Beauty took it but, as she did, she pricked her finger. Instantly, Beauty slumped onto a dusty old bed and fell into a deep sleep.

As soon as Beauty began to sleep, a strange thing happened in the castle. The king and queen, on their thrones, yawned and dozed off. The court jester slumped to the floor and the cook fell asleep in the middle of preparing dinner. Soon, everyone in the castle had drifted off to sleep.

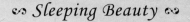

Around the castle moat, green tendrils began to sprout from the ground. In moments, the tendrils grew up and up and twined their way around the castle. Huge, sharp, thorns grew thickly. It was part of the third fairy's magic, to protect Beauty and the castle from harm.

When people in the outside world saw what had happened to the castle, they stayed away. Occasionally, adventurers would come, seeking the riches of the sleeping king, but they were always turned back by the sharp thorns and the castle remained untouched.

One hundred years passed in silence, until a handsome prince rode by and stumbled upon the thorn-covered castle. "I must find out what is inside," said the prince. He drew his sword and cut through the thick tangle of thorns.

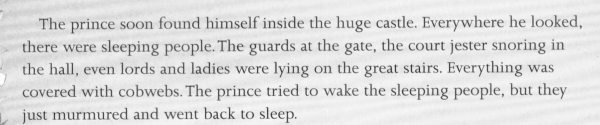

The prince soon found himself inside the huge castle. Everywhere he looked, there were sleeping people. The guards at the gate, the court jester snoring in the hall, even lords and ladies were lying on the great stairs. Everything was covered with cobwebs. The prince tried to wake the sleeping people, but they just murmured and went back to sleep.

As he passed through the Great Hall, the prince saw a little door standing open. It led to a tiny, winding staircase. Climbing the staircase, he found a room in the highest tower of the castle with an old, cobwebbed spinning wheel, standing in one corner. On the dusty bed, lay the most beautiful girl he had ever seen. He leaned over and gave the girl a single kiss. Beauty stirred and opened her eyes. When she saw the prince, she fell instantly in love.

The spell was broken and the silent castle began to stir. The king and queen woke up, the jester started to juggle and the cook began cooking. The whole castle had come back to life. The prince went to the king and asked him for his daughter's hand in marriage.

In no time at all, the people of the castle had recovered from their hundred years' sleep. The prince and Beauty were married and everyone lived happily ever after.

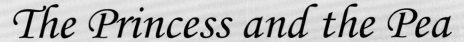

The Princess and the Pea

Once, there lived a prince who wanted to marry. He travelled all around the world and met many princesses, but he didn't fall in love with any of them. Some were too proud and haughty, while others were rude, or thoughtless. "Finding a wife is so hard," the prince sighed. "If only I could meet a princess who was kind and sensitive."

After his travels, the prince returned to his home town, where his parents, the king and queen, greeted him. "Don't worry," the queen said, "I'm sure you'll meet the right princess, one day."

That night, there was a terrible storm. Thunder crashed and lightning flashed. Inside the palace, the king and queen were just about to go to bed when there was a knock at the door. The king opened it to find a pretty young woman standing on the doorstep. She was soaked to the skin.

The queen sat the young woman in front of the fire to dry her clothes. "Why have you come here, my dear?" she asked.
"I am a poor servant girl, looking for work," replied the young woman. "Please don't turn me away."

The prince had heard the knocking and came to see who it was. When he saw the girl, he fell instantly in love with her. The prince sat and talked with the young woman for a long time. "I wish she were a princess," he thought. "I would marry her straight away."

Soon, they were laughing together like old friends. "I was raised by a poor couple," the young woman explained. "They always told me that my real parents were royal, but I never believed them. Now that my foster parents have both died, there is no way to find out," she finished, sadly.

That night, the queen had a bed prepared with many mattresses, piled high, on top of each other. "This girl looks like a princess and she acts like a princess," thought the queen. "She must have royal blood and I think I know how to find out." She placed a single pea under the bottom mattress and sent a servant to fetch the young woman.

The queen showed the young woman into the bedroom and put a ladder against the side of the mattresses. "You can sleep here tonight," she said. The young woman thought it was a very strange way to spend the night. However, she was too polite to complain and climbed up the ladder.

The young women lay down on the mattresses and tried to go to sleep, but it was no good. No matter how she tossed and turned, she could feel something under the mattresses. It kept her awake the whole night. When the sun shone through the windows in the morning, she still felt tired. She climbed down the ladder and went out into the hall.

"Did you have a good night's sleep?" asked the queen.

"No," said the young woman, shyly. "I think there was something under the mattresses, it felt like a hard lump. I was tossing and turning all night." At these words, the queen nodded and smiled to herself.

That afternoon, the queen went for a walk with the prince. "I am in love with the servant girl, mother," he said. "I just wish that she was a princess, instead of a servant girl." The prince looked very sad.

The queen smiled at her son. "Don't worry," she said. "The girl really is a true princess. Only someone with royal blood could be delicate enough to feel a single pea under that many mattresses."

The prince was overjoyed at this happy news. He rushed back into the palace to find the princess. As soon as he saw her, he got down on one knee and asked for her hand in marriage. She accepted gladly, for she had fallen in love with the prince when she first set eyes on him.

The prince and the princess were married in the castle and everyone had a great celebration. The princess never did find out why she had to sleep on so many mattresses, but she and the prince lived happily ever after anyway.

Twelve Dancing Princesses

A king once had twelve daughters. They were good daughters, except for one, very strange thing. Every night, the princesses left their shoes by their beds. Every morning, the shoes would be completely worn out. Whenever the king asked the princesses why this was, they giggled and ran off.

The king spent so much money on new shoes for his daughters, that the kingdom began to run out of money. The king decided that something had to be done. He issued a proclamation throughout the land, "Whoever can find out what happens to my daughters' shoes will become heir to the throne. He may also marry any of my daughters. But whoever fails to find out the secret in three days, will be banished."

One brave knight after another vowed to find out the secret of the twelve princesses. They tried to stay up all night, but when the sun came up each one found that he had drifted into a deep sleep. The shoes were worn out and there was no clue as to how it had happened. These knights were banished, just as the king had promised.

One day, a soldier returned to the kingdom after a long time away.
When he heard about the proclamation, he went to the king. "I will find out
the princesses' secret," said the soldier. "I have spent my life fighting. A few
princesses don't scare me."

While the soldier was walking back from the palace to his cottage, he met
an old, wise woman and told her of his quest. "Here," said the wise woman,
holding out her hands. "Take this cloak."

"What cloak?" asked the soldier.

"It is a cloak of invisibility," said the wise woman.

The soldier held the invisible cloak. Even though he couldn't see it, he could feel its soft material in his hands. "Pretend to be asleep when the princesses call you," said the wise woman. "Then, put on the cloak. However, make sure you don't eat, or drink anything they give you."

The next night, after the princesses had got ready for bed, the soldier stood guard over them. "Take this drink," said the eldest princess, handing the soldier a goblet. "It will warm you through the night." The soldier pretended to drink from the goblet, but he secretly poured it away and pretended to fall fast asleep.

The princesses sat up in bed and looked at the soldier. "Quick," said the eldest princess. "Let's go!" She opened a trap door in the floor and the princesses put on their shoes and went through it. Quickly slipping on the cloak of invisibility, the soldier followed them.

The princesses walked down a stairway into a dark tunnel. The soldier followed too closely and stepped on the youngest princess' dress.

"Someone stepped on my dress!" she said, fearfully.

"Nonsense," said the eldest princess. "Hurry up, the princes are waiting."

The tunnel opened out into a wonderful land, filled with shining trees. As they passed through, the soldier saw that the leaves on the trees were made of silver. The soldier broke off a silver twig and the youngest princess heard the sound. "There is someone here," she said again, but the others told her not to be so silly.

Next, the princesses passed through a land where the trees had leaves made of gold. Then they visited a third land, where the trees had leaves of solid diamonds. The soldier had to shade his eyes, because the trees were so dazzling.

The princesses arrived at a wide, underground lake. There, twelve fairy princes, wearing glittering clothes, waited in twelve little boats. They rowed the princesses across the great lake. The soldier hid in the youngest princess' boat. No one noticed him because the magic cloak made him invisible.

When they reached the far shore, the soldier saw that they had travelled to Fairyland. Music started up from unseen instruments and the princes and the princesses danced all night. When they were tired, they drank from golden goblets.

At last, it was time to return. The soldier made sure he got back to the bedroom first. When the princesses arrived, the soldier pretended to be snoring. "It's a shame that this soldier must be banished when he fails to find out our secret," said the eldest, "but we have been bewitched and there is nothing we can do."

The next night, the soldier followed the princesses again. This time, he took a twig from one of the golden trees. On the third and last night, the soldier followed them and took a twig from a diamond tree. While the princesses danced, the soldier took a goblet and brought it back with him. The next day, the soldier came to the king. "Tell me the princesses' secret," the king said, "or I will banish you like the rest."

"The princesses have been bewitched by twelve fairy princes," said the soldier. When he showed the king and the princesses the twigs and the goblet, the spell on the princesses was broken. The king was no longer angry and hugged his daughters to him. "You may choose any of my daughters to marry," he said to the soldier.

The soldier thought for a long time. "The eldest is my choice," he said. "She is the cleverest of them all." The eldest princess married the soldier gladly and they lived happily ever after.

The Fairy Queen

Once upon a time, a princess had three older sisters who loved to go to balls and parties. The princess wanted to go too, but she was too young. When her sisters were getting ready to go out, the youngest princess would go off by herself and walk around the fields and hills near the castle.

One day, the princess took a different path than usual and found herself in a wooded glade. The sun was setting and it would soon be dark. The princess knew she had to return home soon. Just as she was about to go back, she saw a glimmer nearby. It was coming from inside a ring of grass.

The princess walked towards the ring and saw pretty girls dressed in white with red caps. They were dancing hand-in-hand, round the ring. The princess knew this must be a fairy ring because her grandmother had often told her about them. Suddenly, the girls called to the princess, "Come and join the dance!"

As soon as the princess stepped into the ring, she saw a fine lady on a white horse appear, as if from nowhere. The lady wore a dress that was covered in pale, gleaming jewels. "I am the Fairy Queen," she said. "Come with us to Fairyland. The party is about to start."

The Fairy Queen took the princess into a strange and beautiful forest on the back of her white horse. The fruit hanging in the trees gave off a pale light, and the princess could see fairy folk playing instruments and dancing gracefully to the enchanting music.

There were plates piled high with delicious-looking cakes and candy. The princess reached out to take a cake, but stopped suddenly. She remembered her grandmother telling her that anyone who tasted fairy food, or drink, would be trapped in Fairyland forever.

The princess danced all night and then she said goodbye. "Please, have a sip of some of our special juice before you go," said the Fairy Queen, handing the princess a golden goblet.

The princess refused. "No thank you, Your Majesty," she said, politely. "I have had a wonderful time. You must come and visit my palace soon."

"Thank you for your invitation," said the Fairy Queen. "We will be at your castle tomorrow night, when the clock chimes eight."

There was a sudden whirl of light and sound. The fairy kingdom disappeared and the princess found herself outside her castle, just as the sun was setting. It was as if no time had passed at all. The princess tried to tell her sisters about the Fairy Queen, but they didn't believe her. "You must have been dreaming," they said.

But, the next night, at eight o'clock, the palace doors opened and the Fairy Queen entered the Great Hall, followed by all the fairy folk. They started to play beautiful fairy music that was strange and magical. Soon, the people of the castle were dancing, whirling gracefully around as if bewitched.

The Fairy Queen watched with a smile. "What pretty people," the princess heard her say. "I will take them all home with me to Fairyland."

"This is my fault," thought the princess. "I have to do something!" She raced down to the palace kitchens. There, she found a small piece of brittle candy and made a big hole in it, so that it resembled a ring.

The princess took the candy to the Fairy Queen. "A present for you, Your Majesty," she said, slipping the ring onto the Fairy Queen's finger. As soon as it touched her skin, the ring suddenly crumbled into small candy pieces.

The Fairy Queen licked her finger. "Why, that wasn't a real ring. It was made of sugar. What a strange girl you are. But enough games," said the Fairy Queen, "you are all coming with me to Fairyland."

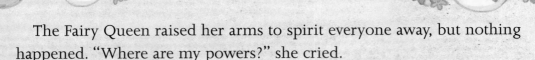

The Fairy Queen raised her arms to spirit everyone away, but nothing happened. "Where are my powers?" she cried.

"My grandmother told me that fairy magic works both ways," said the princess. "Now that you have tasted mortal food, I'm afraid your powers are lost until you return to Fairyland."

The Fairy Queen looked furious, then amused. She nodded. "Fair is fair, Princess. We will go, but remember, Fairyland is always open to you." Then in a flash, the fairies were all gone.

When the princess was old enough to go to the palace balls, everyone noticed that she was the finest dancer of them all. Some said it was because her sisters had taught her, but the princess knew it was because she had once danced all night with the Fairy Queen.